Spectrum Guardian Chronicles

Book One:

Spectrum Guardian: The Prism of Identity

by

Adriano Alamia

For my cousin, Miguel:

Thank you for inspiring me every day.

In your unwavering support and boundless imagination, I found the spark that ignited the world of Luminara. Just as Rory discovered his destiny, you helped me discover the limitless possibilities of storytelling.

This book is a tribute to our shared dreams and the belief that within each of us lies the power to become a guardian of our own multiverse.

With gratitude and love,

Adriano

Table of Contents

Chapter 1

Echoes in the Dark

The city of Luminara never slept; its myriad of lights flickering like stars fallen to earth. Amidst the neon glow and shadowed alleys, Rory felt invisible and glaringly conspicuous. He walked the rain-slicked streets, the multicolored reflections dancing off puddles like fragments of a forgotten rainbow.

Rory had always known he was different, but it wasn't until his fifteenth birthday that he realized how diverse he was. That night, as he lay in his narrow bed at St. Agnes' Orphanage, a surge of unexplained energy rippled through his veins, as vivid and vibrant as the city's lights. It was as if the emotional turmoil that had simmered within him for years had suddenly found a vent, erupting into a spectrum of colors that danced across his skin.

He remembered how the walls of his room glowed, bathed in hues of deep blues, fiery reds, and calming greens, pulsating in tune with his racing heart. Fear mingled with wonder in his wide, tear-filled eyes. He was a canvas of his emotions, a living, breathing prism.

But with this wonder came a crushing loneliness. Rory had always been the odd one out at the orphanage, his quiet demeanor and introspective nature setting him apart from the others. And now, with this strange power burgeoning within him, that gap seemed to widen. He longed for someone to understand and share his secret's bizarre and beautiful terror.

The days that followed were a blur of discovery and concealment. Rory learned that his emotions could change his skin's colors and bend light, create illusions, and even, to his astonishment, form objects out of thin air. He practiced secretly, honing his abilities in the orphanage's abandoned attic, away from prying eyes.

But powers such as these were not meant to stay hidden. One fateful evening, as Rory walked home through the maze of Luminara's streets, he witnessed a mugging in a dimly lit alley. Without thinking, he stepped forward, his emotions flaring. Light coalesced around him, forming a barrier between the mugger and his victim.

"Who are you?" the mugger stammered, stumbling back in fear and awe.

Rory still needs to answer. He didn't know. Who was he? A boy with no past and a bizarre gift? Or was he something more, something meant for more incredible things?

As the mugger fled into the night, the victim, a young woman, looked at Rory with a mixture of gratitude and confusion. "Thank you," she whispered. Rory nodded, his heart pounding from the encounter and realizing he could no longer hide. He was a part of this city, its light and shadow, and maybe he was meant to protect it.

But the truth of who he was and where his powers came from still eluded him. Those answers lay hidden in the depths of Luminara, in the mysteries of his own heart. And Rory, the Spectrum Guardian, was only beginning his journey to find them.

Chapter 2

Colors of Truth

The incident in the alley lingered in Rory's mind like a vivid dream, replaying over and over as he lay awake in his small bed at the orphanage. His room, a stark contrast to the vibrant city outside, felt more confining than ever. The moonlight streamed through the window, casting a pale glow on the walls that once shimmered with his unspoken emotions.

In the stillness of the night, Rory's thoughts wandered to his unknown parents. He imagined them as figures of light and shadow, wondering if they, too, had known the burden and beauty of the powers he now held. The mystery of his lineage was like a locked door in his mind, one he had grown more desperate to open with each passing year.

The following day, Rory's routine remained unchanged. He helped with chores, attended classes, and interacted with the other orphans as little as possible. But inside, a storm of emotions raged, a kaleidoscope of fear, excitement, and an unquenchable thirst for answers.

After the day's duties, Rory returned to his secret refuge – the abandoned attic. The dust motes danced in the slanting light as he practiced his abilities, each burst of color reflecting a fragment of his inner self. He was learning to control the light, to shape it into forms that defied logic – a floating orb, a shimmering shield, even a simple toy that he wished he had owned as a younger child.

But with control came questions. Questions that gnawed at him, demanding answers. Who was he? What was the source of his powers? Rory knew he needed to explore beyond the orphanage's walls to delve into the heart of Luminara.

As evening fell, he made a decision. He would venture into the city's underbelly, where rumors of ancient secrets and hidden powers abounded. Perhaps there, in the forgotten corners and hidden enclaves of Luminara, he could find clues to his past.

Dressed in dark clothes, Rory melted into the shadows of the city. The neon signs and street lamps painted the night in many colors, each hue whispering secrets of the city's soul. He was drawn to the old district, where legend spoke of mystics and seers trafficked in the unknown.

In a narrow, cobblestoned alley, he found what he was looking for – a small, unassuming shop, its windows cluttered with strange artifacts and ancient tomes. The sign above the door read "The Arcanum."

Heart racing, Rory stepped inside. The air was thick with the scent of old books and exotic spices. An older woman sat behind the counter, her eyes sharp and knowing.

"Welcome to The Arcanum, seeker of truths," she said, her voice a melody of hidden depths. "What is it that you wish to find?"

Rory hesitated, then spoke the truth that burned in his heart. "I want to know who I am."

The woman studied him, her gaze piercing through his very soul. "Then your journey has truly begun, Spectrum Guardian," she whispered, a hint of a smile on her lips.

At that moment, Rory knew his life would never be the same. He had entered a world of mysteries and wonders, where his search for identity would lead him to confront the most profound truths of the universe and himself.

Chapter 3

Whispers in the Shadows

The woman's eyes, ancient and wise, seemed to hold galaxies within them. "I am Esmera," she introduced herself, her voice a soft echo in the cramped shop. "And you, Rory, are more than just a boy with unusual gifts."

Rory's heart skipped a beat. "How do you know my name?" he asked, his voice barely a whisper.

Esmera smiled, a knowing, cryptic smile. "In the realms of magic and ancient powers, names are known to those who need to know them," she said, shuffling through her collection of artifacts. "Your powers, they are rare, connected to the emotional Spectrum. Few possess such abilities, and fewer still understand their origins."

Rory's mind raced. "Can you tell me about my parents? Do they have these powers, too?"

The older woman paused, then turned to face him, her expression solemn. "The answers you seek are not easily found. They are woven into the very fabric of Luminara's history. But beware, child, for such knowledge comes at a price."

Rory nodded, determination setting in. "I'll do whatever it takes."

Esmera handed him a small, weathered book. "Start here. This tome speaks of the ancient Guardians, beings of immense power who once walked these streets. You, Rory, may be connected to them more than you realize."

Taking the book, Rory felt a surge of energy pulse through him. The pages seemed to glow under his touch, resonating with the power coursing through his veins.

"Your journey is not just about finding out who you are but also about understanding the responsibility that comes with your powers," Esmera cautioned. Some forces in Luminara seek to harness such power for darker purposes."

Rory looked up, his eyes alight with newfound purpose. "I need to know. I need to understand."

"That is the spirit of a true Guardian," Esmera said with a hint of pride. "But remember, knowledge is only as powerful as the heart that wields it."

As Rory left the shop, the night seemed to embrace him, the city's whispers guiding his steps. He opened the book and began to read, each word illuminating the shadows of his past, drawing him deeper into the labyrinth of his legacy.

The streets of Luminara stretched out before him, both familiar and mysterious. Unknown dangers lurked in the shadows, but Rory felt a newfound strength. He was no longer just an orphan lost in the city's chaos; he was a seeker of truths, a potential guardian of an ancient legacy.

And so, with the weight of history in his hands and the light of determination in his heart, Rory stepped into the night, ready to unravel the mysteries of his birthright and the true extent of his powers.

Chapter 4

The Legacy Unfolds

As Rory delved into the pages of the ancient tome, the words seemed to dance before his eyes, each sentence unveiling secrets long buried. The book spoke of the Spectrum Guardians, a lineage of protectors who wielded the powers of the emotional Spectrum to defend Luminara from unseen threats. The powers manifested differently with each Guardian, shaped by their innermost emotions and experiences.

Realizing that he might be part of this legacy filled Rory with awe and apprehension. Could he, an orphan without knowledge of his heritage, be the next in this line of mystical defenders?

Lost in thought, Rory wandered the labyrinthine streets of Luminara, each step taking him deeper into the city's heart. The old districts, with their cobbled streets and whispering winds, seemed to echo with the tales of the Guardians. It was here that Rory felt closest to the answers he sought.

As he walked, Rory practiced his abilities, the colors shifting and shimmering around him, unseen by the oblivious passersby. He was becoming more adept at controlling his powers; his emotions now channels for the extraordinary light he could wield.

But with this growing mastery came a sense of urgency. Rory knew that understanding his powers was only part of his journey. The other was learning the responsibilities that arrived with them. The book warned of the Eclipsers, shadowy figures who had opposed the Guardians for centuries, seeking to snuff out the light they protected.

When he stumbled upon an unexpected scene, Rory's mind was a whirlwind of thoughts. In a secluded part of the old district, he witnessed a group of cloaked figures surrounding a young girl, their intentions malevolent. Without a second thought, Rory stepped forward, his body igniting with a spectrum of light.

"Leave her alone!" he shouted, his voice echoing with a power he hadn't known he possessed.

The figures turned, surprised by his sudden appearance. One of them, the leader, stepped forward. "Ah, the young Guardian reveals himself," the figure hissed, a chilling smile spreading across his face.

Rory's heart pounded in his chest, but he stood his ground. "I don't know what you're talking about," he said, though deep down, he knew this confrontation was no coincidence.

"You may not know us, but we know you, Rory. Or should I say, Spectrum Guardian?" the leader taunted. "We've been waiting for you to emerge. You see, your light is a threat to our plans."

Rory's mind raced. These Eclipses, they knew about him, about his powers. But how?

The leader raised his hand, and the air around them darkened. "Let's see if you're worthy of your legacy, boy," he sneered.

A battle ensued, the alleyway exploding with light and shadow as Rory fought to protect the girl and himself. His powers, fueled by his emotions, were both his weapon and his shield. The Eclipses were skilled, but Rory's light was blinding and unpredictable.

Ultimately, the cloaked figures retreated into the shadows from whence they came, leaving Rory breathless but victorious. The girl, no older than ten, looked up at him with wide, awe-filled eyes.

"Who are you?" she asked in a trembling voice.

Rory knelt beside her, his light dimming to a soft glow. "Just someone who wants to help," he replied, a small smile tugging at his lips.

As he walked the girl home, Rory knew his life had changed forever. He was no longer just searching for his identity but living it. He was Rory, the Spectrum Guardian of Luminara, and his journey had just begun.

Chapter 5
A Light in the Darkness

After ensuring the young girl's safety, Rory found himself wandering the streets, his mind a tumult of thoughts and emotions. The encounter with the Eclipses had shaken him to his core. They knew him, yet he understood nothing of them. It was a dangerous disadvantage, one he needed to rectify.

Rory's thoughts were interrupted by the soft hum of Luminara at night. With its contrasting shadows and luminescence, the city felt like an extension of itself. The glowing billboards, the dimly lit cafes, and the people lost in their worlds all painted a picture of a beautiful and complex life.

Determined to understand more about the Eclipsers and his role as a Guardian, Rory returned to the Arcanum the next day. Esmera greeted him knowingly as if she had anticipated his return.

"You have encountered the darkness," she stated, more a fact than a question.

"Yes," Rory replied, his voice tinged with frustration. "They knew who I was, but I know nothing about them."

Esmera nodded, her eyes reflecting a depth of knowledge. "The Eclipsers have been enemies of the Guardians for generations. They seek to extinguish the light of the world, believing that in darkness, their power is absolute."

Rory listened as Esmera explained the history of the Guardians and the Eclipses. It was a tale of light and shadow, of protectors who wielded the emotional Spectrum against those who thrived in the absence of light. This ancient struggle had now become his own.

"But why me? Why am I a Guardian?" Rory asked, the weight of his destiny heavy on his shoulders.

Esmera sighed a trace of sorrow in her eyes. "The powers of a Guardian are passed down through bloodlines, often dormant until awakened by strong emotions or events. Though unknown to you, your heritage carries the legacy of the Guardians."

Rory absorbed her words, a sense of responsibility settling over him. He was a part of something much more significant than himself, a lineage that had protected Luminara for centuries.

"Your powers are still raw, unrefined," Esmera continued. "You must learn to harness them, to control the spectrum not just with emotion, but with discipline and will."

She handed him a small, intricately carved box. "Inside, you will find crystals. Each represents an aspect of the emotional Spectrum. Use them to train, to focus your abilities."

Gratefully, Rory took the box, feeling its ancient energy pulsate in his hands. "Thank you, Esmera. I won't let this city down."

As he left the Arcanum, Rory felt a renewed sense of purpose. He had much to learn and a formidable enemy to confront. But he was not alone. The city of Luminara, with all its lights and shadows, stood with him.

That night, in the seclusion of the orphanage attic, Rory opened the box. The crystals glowed softly, each a different color and different emotion. He focused on them individually, feeling his powers respond, ebbing and flowing with the light.

Hours turned into days and days into weeks. Rory trained relentlessly, mastering manipulating and bending light to his will. He learned to create solid light constructs, cloak himself in invisibility, and project his emotions in powerful, tangible ways.

But training was only part of his journey. The Eclipses were still lurking in the shadows, their plans a mystery. Rory knew he needed allies, others who could help him navigate the dangers he had yet to face.

His thoughts turned to his fellow orphans, the people of Luminara, and the friends he had yet to make. In this battle of light and darkness, he would need every ally he could find.

With each day, Rory grew more robust and more confident. He was no longer just an orphan with unanswered questions. He was Spectrum Guardian, a beacon of light in a world shadowed by darkness, ready to face whatever challenges lay ahead.

Chapter 6

Allies in the Shadows

Rory's newfound resolve led him on a path not just of self-discovery but also of building connections. He realized that to face the Eclipsers, he would need more than just his powers; he needed allies, people he could trust.

His first thought was of Mia, a girl at the orphanage who had always been kind to him. With her sharp wit and observant eyes, Mia had a way of understanding people that Rory admired. He decided to confide in her, to reveal his secret, and hope she would stand by him.

It was a fantastic evening when Rory approached Mia in the orphanage's dimly lit standard room. The other children were busy with their activities, paying no mind to the two in their quiet corner.

"Mia," Rory began, his voice low, "there's something I need to tell you about me."

Mia looked at him, her eyes reflecting a mix of curiosity and concern. "What is it, Rory?"

Taking a deep breath, Rory let the colors flow over his hands, a soft display of his powers. Mia's eyes widened in astonishment, but she didn't recoil. Instead, she leaned closer, a sense of wonder in her gaze.

"How are you doing that?" she whispered.

Rory explained everything - his powers, the Eclipses, and his lineage as a Guardian. Mia listened intently, her expression shifting from shock to awe to determination.

"We have to help you," she said firmly. "You can't face this alone."

Rory felt a surge of gratitude. Mia's acceptance and willingness to help strengthened his resolve. Together, they began planning how to gather information about the Eclipsers and their activities in Luminara.

Their first lead came unexpectedly. Mia overheard a conversation about a series of strange occurrences in the city - unexplained shadows, missing people, and a general sense of unease. It was a clue, albeit vague, but it was all they had.

Rory and Mia spent their nights scouring the city, investigating the locations of these occurrences. Rory's powers were crucial in their search, allowing them to remain unseen and gather information without drawing attention.

One night, their investigation led them to an abandoned warehouse in the industrial district. The place had a sinister air, the shadows clinging too tightly to its walls. Rory could feel a pulse of dark energy emanating from within.

Rory's colors flared as they approached, reacting to the evil presence. He turned to Mia, his expression serious. "Stay back. I'll go in alone."

Mia started to protest, but Rory's look of determination stopped her. "Be careful," she said instead, her voice laced with worry.

Rory entered the warehouse, his body glowing softly, illuminating the darkness. Inside, he found more than he had bargained for. The Eclipses were there, gathered around an ancient artifact that pulsed with dark energy. They were chanting, their voices a cacophony of shadows.

Hiding in the shadows, Rory listened, his heart racing. The Eclipses spoke of a plan, a ritual that would plunge Luminara into eternal darkness. The artifact was crucial to their scheme, a relic of old magic that could amplify their powers.

Rory knew he had to act. He couldn't let them succeed. But he also learned he was outnumbered and outmatched. He needed a plan, and he required it fast.

Stepping back into the night, Rory returned to Mia with the information. Together, they realized the gravity of the situation. Luminara was in peril, and they were the only ones who knew.

Rory's thoughts raced. He needed more than just bravery and powers to stop the Eclipses. He required a team, a group of individuals who could help him in this fight.

And so, with a new goal in mind, Rory and Mia set out to find those brave enough, those willing to stand with the Spectrum Guardian against the impending darkness.

Chapter 7

Gathering the Light

The quest to form a team led Rory and Mia through the diverse tapestry of Luminara's neighborhoods, each a different shade in the city's vibrant Spectrum. Rory knew that the individuals they sought needed to be more than just brave; they needed unique skills or knowledge to aid their fight against the Eclipses.

Their first recruit was Lucas, a tech-savvy teenager with a knack for hacking and electronic surveillance. Rory and Mia found him in a small, cluttered workshop in the heart of the city's tech district. Lucas was initially skeptical, but the demonstration of Rory's powers convinced him of the seriousness of the situation. Intrigued by the challenge and the chance to use his skills for a more significant cause, Lucas agreed to join them.

Next was Aria, a young woman with a deep understanding of Luminara's history and lore.

They found her in the city's vast library, her nose buried in ancient texts. Aria was a wealth of knowledge about the city's mystical past, including legends of the Guardians and the Eclipses. Her fascination with the city's hidden secrets made her an invaluable addition to the team.

The last member they sought was more elusive. Rumors spoke of a mysterious figure in the city's underbelly, a master of stealth and information. This figure, known only as "The Shade," was said to be able to obtain unnoticed and undetected information.

Tracking down The Shade was a challenging task. It required combing through the city's shadowy corners and back alleys, following whispers and half-truths. Finally, in a dimly lit tavern hidden away in the oldest part of the city, they found their quarry.

The Shade, a figure cloaked in anonymity, listened to their plea with an unreadable expression. Rory explained their situation, the threat of the Eclipses, and their need for someone with The Shade's particular set of skills. After a long, tense moment, The Shade nodded. No words were spoken, but the message was clear. They were in.

With the team assembled Rory felt a renewed sense of hope. Each member brought something unique, creating a diverse and capable group. They gathered in the attic of the orphanage, which Rory and Mia had converted into a makeshift headquarters.

Lucas set up his equipment, turning the space into a digital surveillance and analysis hub. Aria spread maps and texts, her knowledge of the city's layout and history providing crucial insight. The Shade remained silent, enigmatic, their input sparse but invaluable.

As they planned their next move, Rory felt the weight of leadership settle upon him. He was no longer a lone guardian; he was part of a team, each member relying on his guidance and strength. It was a daunting responsibility but one he was determined to meet.

Their first task was to disrupt the Eclipsers' ritual. Lucas used his hacking skills to pinpoint the ritual's location, while Aria provided historical context that helped them understand its significance. The Shade gathered intelligence on the Eclipsers' movements and defenses.

He arrived the night of the operation. The team, a patchwork of talents and backgrounds, moved through the city's veins, a collective pulse of determination and resolve. As they neared the ritual site, the tension mounted. Rory could feel the dark energy pulsating, starkly contrasting the Spectrum of light he embodied.

The Eclipses were gathered around the ancient artifact, their chants rising into the night. Rory and his team positioned themselves, each ready to play their part in thwarting the dark scheme.

Rory took a deep breath, the colors swirling around him. This was it, the moment of truth. The future of Luminara hung in the balance, and he was the fulcrum upon which it rested. With a nod to his team, he stepped into the light, ready to defend his city and unravel the mysteries of his past.

Chapter 8

The Battle for Light

The night air was tense as Rory and his team approached the ritual site. The Eclipses, cloaked in darkness, were so engrossed in their incantations around the ominous artifact that they didn't immediately notice the arrival of Rory and his allies.

Hidden in the shadows, Lucas began to jam the Eclipsers' communication devices, ensuring they couldn't call for reinforcements. Aria, armed with her extensive knowledge of ancient lore, whispered instructions to Rory about the artifact, believed to be an ancient relic capable of amplifying dark energies.

The Shade, ever elusive, melted into the shadows, moving to flank the Eclipsers and provide an element of surprise. Mia stayed close to Rory, her determined gaze betraying no fear.

Rory took the lead, stepping into the open. His appearance, radiant with multicolored light, momentarily startled the Eclipses. The group leader, a tall figure shrouded in a dark cloak, sneered at Rory.

"The Spectrum Guardian comes to challenge us," he mocked. "You are too late. The ritual is almost complete."

Rory responded not with words but with action. He focused, channeling his emotions into a brilliant display of light—beams of vibrant energy shot forth, disrupting the ritual and causing chaos among the Eclipses.

Lucas's technical prowess then came into play. He hacked into the nearby streetlights, causing them to flicker erratically, further disorienting the Eclipses. Aria, chanting an ancient incantation, weakened the artifact's dark aura, diminishing its power.

The Shade emerged from the shadows, taking down Eclipsers swiftly and silently. Their movements were like a dance, a shadow weaving through the night.

Though Mia lacked supernatural powers, she showed her bravery by helping to disrupt the ritual site, overturning the Eclipsers' equipment, and scattering their dark talismans.

The battle was intense, with light and darkness clashing in a tumultuous symphony. Rory, at the center, felt his emotions surge. Anger, fear, and hope fed his powers, creating a dazzling display of chromatic energy. He was the embodiment of the Spectrum, a beacon in the darkness.

The Eclipses fought back with renewed enthusiasm, realizing their ritual was compromised. Their leader, adept in dark magic, hurled shadowy bolts towards Rory. The young Guardian countered with shields of light, each impact sending ripples of color through the air.

As the battle reached its crescendo, Rory knew what to do. Focusing all his energy, he directed a concentrated light beam toward the artifact. The beam pierced the darkness, striking the relic with a blinding explosion of color.

The ritual was broken, and the artifact shattered. The Eclipses' power source was destroyed, and they retreated into the night, their plans foiled. The leader gave Rory a vicious look before vanishing into the shadows.

As calm returned, Rory and his team looked around at the aftermath. They had won, but this was only the beginning. The Eclipsers would not give up so quickly, and the mystery of Rory's heritage and the full extent of his powers remained unsolved.

Yet, in that moment, Rory felt a sense of accomplishment and unity. He looked at his friends – Lucas, Aria, The Shade, and Mia – and realized they were strong together. They were a team, a family bound not by blood but by a shared purpose.

"We did it," Mia said, her voice filled with relief and pride.

"Yes," Rory agreed, the colors around him fading to a soft glow. "But this is just the first step. We have a long journey ahead."

As they left the site, the city of Luminara spread out before them, its lights twinkling like stars in the night sky. Rory knew that as long as the city shone with light, he would protect the Spectrum Guardian, a beacon of hope in a world of shadows.

Chapter 9

Shadows of the Past

The victory at the ritual site was a turning point for Rory and his team. They had proven capable of standing against the Eclipses, but the battle had also raised many questions. The most pressing was the origin of the dark artifact and how it connected to the Eclipsers' plans to engulf Luminara in darkness.

In the days following the confrontation, the team regrouped in their attic headquarters to piece together information. Aria pored over ancient texts, seeking references to similar artifacts and rituals. Lucas continued his surveillance and data analysis, tapping into city networks for signs of Eclipse activity.

The ever-enigmatic Shade brought in whispers from the streets – rumors of hidden places and forgotten lore that might hold the key to understanding the Eclipsers' motives. Mia, ever the practical one, organized their findings and ensured the team remained focused and coordinated.

Rory, meanwhile, delved deeper into his powers. The battle had shown him the potential of his abilities and the need for greater control and understanding. He practiced daily, refining his control over the light Spectrum, each color representing a different emotion and energy.

It was during one of these training sessions that Rory experienced a breakthrough. As he focused on a beam of pure, brilliant light, he felt a connection to something ancient and powerful – a presence that seemed to echo from the depths of his soul.

Startled, Rory shared this experience with Esmera at the Arcanum. The wise older woman listened intently, her eyes reflecting a deep knowledge.

"You are tapping into the legacy of the Guardians," she explained. "Each Guardian is connected to their predecessors, drawing strength from their experiences and wisdom.

This connection is more than just power; it links to the Guardians' history."

Rory absorbed her words, a sense of awe washing over him. He was part of a lineage that spanned centuries, each Guardian a protector of light against the encroaching darkness.

With this revelation came a new determination. Rory knew he needed to learn more about his predecessors to understand their struggles and victories. Such knowledge could be crucial in their fight against the Eclipses.

The team's research led them to an ancient site in the heart of Luminara – the ruins of what was the first Guardian's sanctuary. Hidden beneath the city, it was a place of power and mystery.

Armed with this information, Rory and his team ventured into the depths of Luminara. The journey through the underground passages was treacherous, filled with traps and ancient protections left by the Guardians of old.

As they navigated the labyrinthine tunnels, the city's history and the Guardians seemed alive. Murals adorned the walls, depicting battles of light against darkness, and statues of previous Guardians stood sentinel in the silent corridors.

Finally, they reached the heart of the sanctuary – a vast chamber illuminated by a soft, ethereal light. In the center stood an ancient pedestal, upon which rested a crystal similar to those Esmera had given Rory.

The crystal began to glow as Rory approached, resonating with the power coursing through him. He reached out, and as his fingers touched the crystal, a flood of visions and memories washed over him. He saw the faces of Guardians long past and felt their joys and sorrows, battles and triumphs.

The experience was overwhelming, but within it lay the wisdom of generations. Rory emerged from the vision with a deeper understanding of his powers and purpose. He also gleaned valuable insights into the Eclipses – their origins entwined with the Guardians in a long-forgotten schism.

With this newfound knowledge, Rory and his team emerged more united and determined from the sanctuary than ever. They now knew that the battle against the Eclipses was not just a fight for the present but a continuation of an age-old struggle between light and darkness.

As they walked back through the streets of Luminara, the city seemed different to Rory. It was not just a place he called home; it was a legacy he had inherited, a beacon of light he swore to protect. And he would do so, with every fiber of his being, as the Spectrum Guardian.

Chapter 10

The Web of Darkness

Reinvigorated by their discoveries, Rory and his team intensified their efforts to unravel the Eclipsers' schemes. The knowledge gained from the Guardian's sanctuary offered new perspectives, revealing the depth and complexity of the conflict they were engaged in.

Lucas's skills were crucial in this phase. He dove into Luminara's digital underworld, tracing encrypted communications and shadowy transactions that hinted at the Eclipsers' network. His discoveries painted a picture of a vast, interconnected web with threads stretching across the city and beyond.

Aria, meanwhile, delved into the historical connections between the Guardians and the Eclipses. She uncovered tales of a bitter betrayal centuries ago, a schism within the ranks of the Guardians that gave birth to the Eclipses. This ancient feud was the genesis of the enduring conflict between light and darkness.

The Shade's contributions were more enigmatic but no less valuable. They infiltrated the darkest corners of Luminara, gathering whispers and rumors that provided clues to the Eclipsers' current plans. Through their efforts, the team learned of a gathering of Eclipser leaders scheduled to take place in a hidden location within the city.

With this information, Rory and his team devised a plan to infiltrate the gathering and learn more about the Eclipse's intentions. It was a risky operation, requiring stealth and precision. The Shade would take the lead, guiding them through the shadows to their destination.

The night of the operation, the team moved through the city like wraiths, unseen and unheard. The Shade led them through a maze of back alleys and forgotten passages, their knowledge of the city's underbelly proving invaluable.

As they neared the location of the gathering, Rory felt a surge of apprehension. This was their chance to strike at the heart of the Eclipsers' network, to unravel their plans and potentially weaken their grip on Luminara. But the danger was immense, the risk of discovery high.

The meeting place was an abandoned warehouse, its exterior unassuming, but the energy pulsating within was anything but ordinary. Dark, oppressive waves emanated from the structure, starkly contrasting the vibrant Spectrum surrounding Rory.

Lucas set up a surveillance perimeter, hacking into nearby security systems to provide them with eyes and ears around the warehouse. Aria and Mia stayed with him, ready to deliver support and relay information as needed.

Rory and The Shade approached the warehouse, their movements cloaked in shadows. Inside, the Eclipses gathered, their voices a low, ominous murmur in the darkness.

Hiding in the rafters, Rory and The Shade listened as the Eclipses discussed their plans. They spoke of an impending event, a ritual that would plunge the city into eternal night, erasing the Guardians' legacy forever.

The stakes were higher than Rory had imagined - it was a battle for control of Luminara, a fight for its soul.

As the meeting continued, Rory felt a growing sense of urgency. They needed to act to disrupt the Eclipsers' plans before it was too late. But a confrontation was too risky with so many Eclipsers present.

In a whispered conversation, Rory and The Shade formulated a new plan. They would sabotage the warehouse, creating a distraction that would scatter the Eclipsers and buy them time to investigate further.

With careful precision, Rory used his powers to manipulate the light within the warehouse, creating illusions and distractions. The Shade moved like a ghost, setting traps and sowing confusion among the Eclipses.

The operation was a success. The Eclipses were thrown into disarray, and their meeting was disrupted. As they fled the warehouse, Rory and his team gathered crucial documents and artifacts left behind in the chaos.

With this new information, they retreated into the night, their mission accomplished, but the threat was far from over. The Eclipses were planning something catastrophic, and time was running out.

As they regrouped in their headquarters, Rory felt the weight of responsibility on his shoulders. He was the Spectrum Guardian, the protector of Luminara's light. And he would do whatever it took to thwart the darkness that threatened his city.

Chapter 11

The Countdown Begins

After the warehouse infiltration, Rory and his team worked tirelessly to decipher the documents and artifacts they had secured. The information painted a grim picture: the Eclipsers planned to perform a dark ritual during the upcoming lunar Eclipse, amplifying their powers and casting a shadow over Luminara.

According to the documents, the ritual required three ancient artifacts, one of which was the shattered relic from the previous encounter. The other two were still at large, hidden somewhere in the city. The Eclipses were close to obtaining them; if they succeeded, the consequences would be catastrophic.

Time was of the essence. Rory and his team divided their efforts to cover more ground. Lucas and Mia focused on tracking the Eclipsers' movements and communications, attempting to pinpoint the locations of the remaining artifacts. The Shade delved deeper into the city's underbelly, gathering intelligence from the shadowy corners of Luminara.

Aria's expertise in ancient lore became invaluable. She identified the two remaining artifacts: the Orb of Shadows, a sphere capable of absorbing light, and the Mirror of Night, a reflective surface that could turn any light into darkness. Both were steeped in dark magic and posed a significant threat in the hands of the Eclipses.

Meanwhile, Rory continued to hone his powers. The visions from the ancient sanctuary had unlocked new facets of his abilities. He discovered he could not only manipulate light but also sense the presence of darkness. This skill would be crucial in locating the artifacts.

The team's efforts led them to the city's historic district, where the Orb of Shadows rumored to hide. The area was a labyrinth of old buildings and narrow streets, echoing

Luminara's past. The atmosphere was heavy with the weight of history, each stone and corner whispering tales of days gone by.

Navigating the district was challenging, with the Eclipses fortifying the area with traps and dark enchantments. Rory's ability to sense darkness guided them through the hazards, his light a beacon in the oppressive gloom.

After a tense journey, they located the Orb of Shadows in an ancient crypt beneath an old cathedral—the orb, a sphere of pure obsidian, pulsed with evil energy. As Rory reached out to claim it, a trap was triggered, unleashing a swarm of shadowy entities.

The battle was fierce. Rory and his team fought bravely, their light clashing with the darkness. Lucas used his gadgets to disrupt the entities' form while Mia provided tactical support. Aria chanted incantations that weakened the shadows, and The Shade fought with silent, deadly precision.

In the end, they emerged victorious, the Orb of Shadows secured. But the victory was short-lived. The Eclipsers, alerted to their presence, converged on the district, their numbers overwhelming.

A retreat was their only option. As they navigated out of the historic district, Rory's mind raced with the realization that the final artifact, the Mirror of Night, was still unaccounted for. The lunar Eclipse was mere days away, and the clock was ticking.

They returned to their headquarters battered but not broken. The Orb of Shadows was safe, but the Mirror of Night remained a mystery. The team poured over the documents again, searching for clues to lead them to the final artifact.

As Rory studied the ancient texts, a sense of urgency gripped him. The fate of Luminara rested in their hands. The Eclipsers' ritual had stopped, and the Mirror of Night had to be found.

With determination set in his heart and the light of the Guardians flowing through his veins, Rory prepared for the final phase of their mission. The battle against darkness was reaching its climax, and he would stand at the forefront, a beacon of hope in the impending Eclipse.

Chapter 12

The Eclipse of Destiny

The days leading up to the lunar Eclipse were a blur of activity. Rory and his team left no stone unturned in their search for the Mirror of Night. The sense of urgency was palpable; the fate of Luminara hung in the balance.

Lucas's technological prowess was crucial during this time. He set up a city-wide monitoring system, using every available camera and sensor to track Eclipser movements. His screens lit up the attic with a constant data flow, creating a digital map of the ongoing chess game between light and darkness.

Mia took charge of logistics, coordinating their efforts with precision and efficiency. Her clear-headedness and strategic thinking kept the team focused and effective despite the mounting pressure.

The Shade continued to be an invaluable asset. Their network of informants provided real-time updates on Eclipser activity. Their ability to gather information from the city's darkest corners was unmatched, shedding light on the Eclipsers' elusive maneuvers.

Aria's knowledge of ancient lore and intuitive understanding of mystical artifacts guided them through the cryptic clues left in old texts and legends. She deduced that the Mirror of Night was likely hidden in the city's oldest quarter, a place steeped in history and magic.

Meanwhile, Rory felt a deepening connection to his Guardian lineage. His powers were reaching new heights, the spectruSpectrumht responding to his emotions and will with increasing sensitivity. He practiced relentlessly, mastering the nuances of his abilities and preparing for the inevitable confrontation with the Eclipses.

As the lunar Eclipse approached, a breakthrough came. The Shade obtained a crucial piece of intelligence – the location of the Mirror of Night. It was hidden in an ancient tower in the heart of the old quarter, shrouded in myths and guarded by dark enchantments.

The team mobilized; their plan was clear. They would infiltrate the tower, retrieve the Mirror, and disrupt the Eclipsers' ritual before the Eclipse peaked. The stakes were high, but they were ready.

On the night of the Eclipse, the city of Luminara seemed to hold its breath. The streets were eerily quiet, the usual hum of life muted under the weight of anticipation. The sky above was a tapestry of stars, the moon a glowing orb soon to be shrouded in shadow.

Rory and his team made their way to the ancient tower; their movements were swift and silent. The old quarter was a maze of narrow streets and towering buildings, their shadows long and deep under the moonlight.

The tower loomed before them, its spire piercing the night sky. The air around it was thick with dark energy, the Eclipsers' magic a tangible force. Rory could feel the darkness pulsing, starkly contrasting the light within him.

They breached the tower's defenses, Lucas disabling ancient traps with his gadgets, Aria countering dark spells with her enchantments. The Shade led the way, their knowledge of stealth and infiltration proving invaluable.

As they ascended the tower, the Eclipse began. The moon slowly darkened, a shadow creeping across its surface. The ritual was starting, and time was running out.

They reached the chamber where the Mirror of Night was kept. It was a room of mirrors, each reflecting the moon's fading light in eerie, distorted ways. In the center stood the Mirror of Night, a large, obsidian surface that absorbed light, leaving only darkness in its wake.

The Eclipses, led by their enigmatic leader, were already there, their ritual underway. The room was alive with dark energy, the air crackling with power.

Rory stepped forward, the light of the Guardians shining brightly around him. "It ends now," he declared, his voice echoing in the chamber.

A fierce battle ensued, light clashing with darkness in a dance of ancient powers. Rory and his team fought valiantly; their skills and resolve tested to the limit.

Lucas disrupted the Eclipsers' magical constructs with his devices, creating openings for the others. Mia, armed with weapons of light, struck with precision and agility. Aria's chants weakened the dark enchantments, her voice a beacon in the gloom. The Shade moved like a shadow, taking down Eclipsers with swift, silent strikes.

Rory faced the Eclipser leader, their powers colliding in a vortex of light and shadow. The leader was influential, his mastery of darkness a formidable force. But Rory's connection to the Guardians, his control over the Spectrum, gave him the edge.

As the Eclipse peaked, Rory unleashed a torrent of chromatic energy, a rainbow of light that pierced the darkness. The Mirror of Night shattered under the assault, its fragments scattered like stars.

The ritual was broken, and the Eclipsers' plan was foiled. The remaining Eclipsers retreated into the night, their leader vanquished.

As the moon emerged from the shadow, bathing the chamber in soft, silver light, Rory and his team stood victorious. They had saved Luminara from eternal darkness, the city's light preserved.

As they descended the tower in the aftermath, Rory felt a profound connection to the city and its people. He was their protector, the Spectrum Guardian, a legacy of light in a world that sometimes veered too close to darkness.

The battle was won, but Rory knew this was not the end. The Eclipses were still out there, and he would be ready. He was Rory, the Spectrum Guardian of Luminara, and his journey was only beginning.

Chapter 13

A New Dawn

The shattered ritual's aftermath marked a victory for Rory and his team and a turning point for the city of Luminara. The night of the Eclipse, he symbolized resilience and hope, a testament to the light prevailing over darkness.

In the days following the battle, Rory felt a change within himself and the city. He walked the streets of Luminara, no longer an invisible orphan but as a guardian whose actions had resonated through every alley and avenue. People spoke of the Spectrum Guardian, a mysterious figure who had saved the city from an eternal night. Rory listened to these stories, a sense of pride mingling with the weight of responsibility that now rested on his shoulders.

His team, too, felt the shift. With his tech expertise, Lucas had become a guardian of the city's digital realm, preventing malicious cyber activities and keeping a vigilant eye on any Eclipser remnants. With her strategic mind and newfound combat skills, Mia continued to work alongside Rory, a loyal ally in the ongoing fight against darkness.

Aria's deep knowledge of the city's lore and history had made her an invaluable resource. She delved deeper into the archives, uncovering more about the Guardians' legacy and the possible future threats Rory might face.

The Shade, ever enigmatic, continued their work in the shadows. They were a crucial ally in gathering intelligence and maintaining a network of informants that kept Rory informed of any undercurrents of darkness within the city.

As for Rory, the battle had deepened his connection to his powers. He discovered new aspects of his abilities, learning to harness the Spectrum in more intricate and powerful ways. He continued to train, pushing his powers' boundaries and preparing for future threats.

Esmera, the wise keeper of the Arcanum, became a mentor to Rory, guiding him in understanding the deeper aspects of his role as a Guardian. She taught him about the balance of light and dark, the importance of emotional control, and the history of the Guardians that came before him.

But with the Eclipsers' defeat, new challenges emerged. The city, having witnessed the existence of magic and supernatural forces, grappled with this new reality. Rory found himself not just fighting against dark forces but helping the city adapt to a world where such elements were no longer just myths and legends.

The media sought to uncover the identity of the Spectrum Guardian. Still, Rory maintained his anonymity, believing that his effectiveness lay in being a symbol rather than a public figure. However, the people of Luminara still had to start speculating and creating their own stories about who he might be.

Meanwhile, the shattered remnants of the Eclipsers regrouped, their defeat only fueling their resolve. Rory knew they would strike again, driven by their belief in darkness. But he also learned that he and his team were ready, a united front against any force threatening the light of Luminara.

As Rory stood atop a building overlooking the city, the skyline of Luminara spread out before him; he reflected on his journey. From an orphan with an unknown past to the protector of a town, his life had changed in ways he could never have imagined. The city's lights twinkled below, each a beacon of hope, a reminder of the light he fought to protect.

In the distance, the moon hung low, a reminder of the night when he had stood against the darkness. Rory knew his journey as the Spectrum Guardian was far from over. There were still mysteries to face, dangers to face, and darkness to overcome.

But for now, he savored the peace that had settled over Luminara. He was Rory, the Spectrum Guardian, a symbol of light in a world that sometimes dwelled too much in the shadows. And as long as the city needed him, he would be there, a guardian of light, a beacon at night.

Chapter 14

The Veil of Secrets

The peace that had descended on Luminara in the aftermath of the Eclipse was fragile. Beneath the surface, secrets and mysteries swirled, hinting at deeper truths yet uncovered. This period was one of reflection and preparation for Rory, now firmly established as the Spectrum Guardian.

Witnessing the supernatural firsthand, the city was abuzz with questions and theories. Some saw Rory as a hero, a beacon of hope. Others were skeptical, wary of the powers that had been revealed. This divide in public opinion created a new dynamic in the city, one that Rory had to navigate carefully.

Amidst this backdrop, Rory continued to explore the extent of his powers. His connection to the emotional Spectrum was strengthened, and he discovered new ways to harness his abilities. He learned to manipulate light and perceive the emotions of others, a skill that proved both a blessing and a burden.

As Rory grappled with these developments, a new challenge emerged. A series of mysterious disappearances began to plague the city. The victims seemed to vanish without a trace, leaving no clues behind. The disappearances were sporadic, with no apparent pattern or connection between the victims.

Rory and his team immediately began investigating. Lucas set up a city-wide surveillance net, sifting through mountains of data for any anomaly. Mia coordinated with the city's law enforcement, providing assistance and insight. Aria delved into the city's mystical history, searching for any past incidents that might shed light on the current situation.

The Shade took to the streets, their network of informants proving invaluable in gathering information from the city's darker corners. They uncovered rumors of a shadowy figure seen near the locations of several disappearances. This clue offered a possible lead.

Driven by a sense of responsibility, Rory patrolled the city at night, his senses attuned to any sign of the perpetrator or the missing citizens. His presence in the streets became a comforting sight for many, a symbol of protection against the unknown.

The breakthrough came when Rory encountered the shadowy figure during patrols. The figure, cloaked in darkness, possessed an aura of malice that sent shivers down Rory's spine. A confrontation ensued, a flurry of light and shadow, revealing the figure's abilities to manipulate darkness in a way that mirrored Rory's control of light.

The figure escaped, but the encounter left Rory with more questions than answers. Who was this new adversary? Were they responsible for the disappearances? And, most importantly, what was their motive?

The team doubled their efforts, piecing together the information they had gathered. They discovered that each victim had a connection to the city's mystical heritage, either through their work or their family lineage. This connection suggested that the disappearances were part of a more sinister plan.

As they delved deeper into the mystery, Rory felt the burden of his role as the Spectrum Guardian. The city's safety rested on his shoulders, and the threat of this new adversary loomed large. But Rory was not alone. His team stood with him, each member committed to unraveling the mystery and protecting Luminara.

The city's blend of modernity and ancient magic was a nexus of mysteries and wonders. Rory knew that the key to solving the disappearances lay in understanding the city's hidden history, the secrets buried in its shadows.

Rory and his team were drawn into a web of secrets and lies as the story unfolded. This puzzle spanned the breadth of Luminara's history. Each clue they uncovered led them deeper into the heart of darkness, a journey that would test their resolve and reveal truths that had long been hidden.

In the city's shadows, a battle was brewing, pitting the Spectrum Guardian's light against the darkness of an unknown foe. The fate of the missing citizens hung in the balance, and Rory knew that he would do whatever it took to bring them home.

Chapter 15

Echoes of the Forgotten

As the investigation into the disappearances deepened, Rory and his team were entangled in a web of ancient mysteries and modern-day intrigue. The city of Luminara, with its rich history steeped in magic and hidden lore, held secrets that were slowly coming to light.

Aria's research into the city's mystical past revealed a forgotten chapter in Luminara's history. Centuries ago, a secret society known as the "Order of the Veil" had operated in the shadows, guardians of arcane knowledge and protectors against dark forces. However, their existence had been erased from history, and their legacy was lost to time.

The connection between the Order of the Veil and the current disappearances was a puzzle. Aria theorized that the victims, all connected to the city's mystical heritage, could be descendants of the Order's members. This connection suggested that the shadowy figure and the disappearances were part of an attempt to revive or exploit the ancient Order's secrets.

Using his technical expertise, Lucas traced patterns in the shadowy figure's movements, leading them to a series of hidden locations across the city. These locations were marked with ancient symbols associated with the Order of the Veil, linking the current events to the long-forgotten society.

The Shade, through their network, gathered rumors of a rising power within the city's underworld, one that sought to harness the mystical energies of Luminara for unknown purposes. This new player was elusive, always one step ahead, their identity shrouded in mystery.

Rory, driven by a sense of duty to protect the city, patrolled these locations, hoping to intercept the shadowy figure and uncover more about their motives. His encounters with the figure were brief and inconclusive, but Rory's understanding of his adversary grew with each confrontation.

The figure was adept at using dark magic, and their powers mirrored Rory's own. This realization made Rory wonder about the nature of his powers and the true extent of the spectrum of light and dark.

One night, during a patrol, Rory stumbled upon a hidden chamber beneath the city streets, an ancient sanctuary of the Order of the Veil. He found relics and tomes that spoke of a ritual to seal away a great darkness that the Order had performed centuries ago.

The pieces of the puzzle began to fall into place. The shadowy figure was attempting to undo the ritual of the Order, to unleash the sealed darkness upon Luminara. The victims, descendants of the Order's members, were vital to completing this counter-ritual.

Armed with this knowledge, Rory and his team devised a plan to stop the figure and prevent the resurgence of the ancient darkness. They would need to protect the remaining descendants and find a way to counter the figure's magic.

The team split up, each member tasked with a crucial part of the plan. Lucas and Mia worked on developing technology to counter the dark magic. At the same time, Aria delved into the Order's rituals to find a way to reinforce the ancient seal.

The Shade continued to gather intelligence, which was crucial in predicting the figure's next move. Meanwhile, Rory focused on protecting the descendants and confronting the shadowy figure.

As the final confrontation approached, the city of Luminara braced itself. The eclipse had shown the citizens the existence of magic and the supernatural. Still, this new threat was more – an echo of the city's forgotten past, a reminder that some secrets should remain hidden.

Standing as the Spectrum Guardian, Rory knew the battle ahead would be unlike any he had faced. It was a fight against an adversary and a struggle to protect Luminara's soul.

The night of the final confrontation arrived, and the city was enveloped in tense anticipation. In the depths of the ancient sanctuary, Rory and his team faced the shadowy figure, the fate of the city hanging in the balance.

The clash was a spectacle of light and darkness, a battle of wills and powers that shook the city's foundations. At the heart of the storm, Rory fought with the strength of his lineage, the light of the Guardians shining brightly against the encroaching shadows.

As the battle raged, Rory realized that the true power lay not in the light or the darkness but in the balance between them. With this understanding, he could turn the tide, countering the figure's magic and reinforcing the ancient seal.

The defeated figure vanished into the shadows, their plans thwarted. The descendants were safe, and the darkness was contained once more.

In the aftermath, as dawn broke over Luminara, the city changed. The past secrets had been revealed, and the balance of light and Dark had been restored.

Standing atop the sanctuary, Rory looked out over the city. He had faced the echoes of the forgotten and emerged victorious. But he knew his role as the Spectrum Guardian was far from over. The city would always have secrets and shadows lurking in its corners.

But as long as there was light in Luminara, as long as there were those who stood against the darkness, the city would endure. And Rory, the Spectrum Guardian, would be there, a protector, a beacon, a guardian of the light.

Chapter 16

The Light Beyond Shadows

In the wake of the confrontation with the shadowy figure and the resealing of the ancient darkness, Rory's role as the Spectrum Guardian took on new dimensions. The city of Luminara, now more aware of its mystical heritage, looked to Rory not just as a protector but also as a bridge between the ordinary and the extraordinary.

The revelation of the Order of the Veil and the thwarted resurgence of ancient darkness had stirred up the city's hidden world. Other mystical factions and solitary practitioners, previously operating in secrecy, began to emerge, seeking alliances or challenging the established Order.

Rory found himself at the center of this evolving tapestry of magic and power. His unique abilities and role as the Guardian made him a figure of interest, respect, and sometimes envy. Navigating this new landscape required diplomacy and a deeper understanding of the city's magical community.

Amidst these developments, a new challenge emerged. A series of arcane disturbances began to ripple across Luminara, disrupting the flow of magic and causing chaos in both the mystical and mundane realms. These disturbances were random and volatile, creating a sense of unease among the city's inhabitants.

Rory and his team embarked on a mission to uncover the source of these disturbances. Lucas's analytical skills were vital in tracking the disturbances' patterns. At the same time, Aria's knowledge of magical lore helped decipher their nature.

Mia coordinated their efforts with the city's authorities, ensuring a cohesive response to the incidents. The Shade, with their network of informants and their understanding of the city's darker corners, provided invaluable insights into the possible origins of the disturbances.

As they delved into the investigation, Rory's powers again proved crucial. His connection to the emotional spectrum allowed him to sense the ebb and flow of the disturbances, guiding their efforts to pinpoint their source.

Their search led them to an ancient ruin beneath the city, a remnant of a time when Luminara was a nexus of magical energies. The ruin, long forgotten, had been awakened by the recent events, its dormant powers now unleashed and uncontrolled.

In the heart of the ruin, they discovered a nexus point, a convergence of ley lines that channeled magical energy throughout the city. The nexus had become destabilized, its energies thrown into chaos by the resealing of the ancient darkness and the resurgence of the city's mystical activity.

The team realized that stabilizing the nexus was crucial to restoring balance in Luminara. The task, however, was fraught with danger. The energies were volatile, and the slightest misstep could exacerbate the situation.

Drawing on his deepening connection to the Guardians' legacy, Rory stabilized the nexus. He delved into the core of the ruin, his body aglow with the spectrum of light, each color representing a facet of his powers and emotions.

The process was intense and demanding. Rory had to harmonize his energies with the chaotic flow of the nexus. This task required immense concentration and control. As he worked, the colors around him swirled in a mesmerizing dance, a visual symphony of light and emotion.

After a tense and exhaustive effort, Rory succeeded. The nexus stabilized, its energies flowing smoothly once again. The disturbances across the city ceased, and a sense of calm returned to Luminara.

The achievement was a testament to Rory's growth as the Spectrum Guardian. He had not only protected the city from physical threats but had also restored its mystical balance.

As Rory emerged from the ruin, his team waiting for him, he knew that his journey was far from over. Luminara was a city of light and shadows, its mysteries deep and ever-evolving. As its Guardian, he would face whatever challenges came next, armed with his powers, allies, and unwavering commitment to protect the city he loved.

The city of Luminara, bathed in the soft glow of dawn, stood as a beacon of hope and resilience. And Rory, the Spectrum Guardian, stood as its protector, symbolizing the light that shines even in the darkest times.

Chapter 17

The Threads of Fate

Following stabilizing the magical nexus, Luminara entered a period of relative calm. However, in a city as steeped in mystery as Luminara, peace was often a precursor to the storms on the horizon. For Rory, now more attuned to the ebbs and flows of the city's magical undercurrents, this period was one of vigilance and growth.

The Spectrum Guardian's role in the city had evolved significantly. Rory was a protector of the physical realm and a steward of the mystical balance that Luminara now openly embraced. His presence symbolized coexistence between the ordinary and the extraordinary, inspiring a new generation of Luminara's inhabitants.

However, new challenges emerged as the city awoke to its mystical heritage. The magical community, once hidden, began to exert its influence, leading to a shift in the city's dynamics. Factions with differing ideologies and objectives sought to sway the balance of power in their favor.

Amidst this backdrop, Rory and his team faced a new problem. A series of cryptic messages began appearing across the city, etched in light on the walls of buildings, visible only at night. The messages spoke of an impending event, a convergence that would alter the course of Luminara's destiny.

Aria, with her extensive knowledge of mystical lore, recognized the language of the messages as an ancient dialect used by the Order of the Veil. She deduced that the messages were warnings, hinting at the awakening of an ancient entity long believed to be a myth.

Lucas's analytical mind was vital in deciphering the messages' locations and timings, revealing a pattern that formed a sigil over the city map. This sigil, a complex array of lines and circles, was a magical construct of significant power. Its purpose was unclear but undoubtedly linked to the foretold convergence.

Mia coordinated efforts to monitor these locations, working closely with the city authorities to manage the growing public curiosity and concern. Her leadership and strategic planning were instrumental in maintaining Order amidst the rising tide of mysticism and speculation.

The Shade delved into the city's shadows, gathering intelligence from the hidden corners of Luminara. Their findings pointed to a surge in magical activity, with various groups and individuals attempting to harness the growing energies for their own purposes.

Rory, meanwhile, faced the daunting task of unraveling the mystery of the convergence. His connection to the emotional spectrum allowed him to sense the shifts in the city's magical fabric, guiding him in his quest to understand the nature of the threat.

As the date of the convergence approached, the city braced itself. Magical energies pulsed through Luminara, the veil between the mundane and the mystical thinner than ever. Rory and his team prepared for whatever lay ahead, knowing that the city's fate rested in their hands.

The night of the convergence arrived, and the city of Luminara was bathed in an ethereal glow. Now fully activated, the sigil pulsed with power; its lines and circles mapped a long-forgotten location.

Rory, guided by the sigil and his instincts, led his team to an ancient site beneath the city, where the boundaries of time and space were blurred. Here, the convergence would reach its apex, the awakening of the ancient entity imminent.

In the depths of this site, they encountered the entity, a being of immense power and age. It was a Guardian from a bygone era, a predecessor of Rory's lineage, trapped in a state of suspended animation but now stirring back to consciousness.

The disoriented and confused entity threatened the city. Its awakening had been manipulated, and its powers were a beacon for those who sought to exploit Luminara's mystical energies. Facing a Guardian of the past, Rory had to find a way to communicate, calm the entity, and prevent a catastrophe.

The confrontation was a clash of light and wills, a testament to Rory's growth as the Spectrum Guardian. He reached out to the entity, his light intertwining with the ancient Guardian's, a dance of colors and emotions that spanned the ages.

Rory calmed the entity through this connection, easing its confusion and fear. He learned of the entity's past, battles fought, and sacrifices made, a legacy Rory carries forward.

The convergence ended with the entity's awakening resolved and its power contained. The sigil faded away as the magical energies dispersed. Luminara was safe once again; its fate averted from a path that could have led to ruin.

In the aftermath, as dawn broke over the city, Rory and his team reflected on the events. They had faced a challenge that bridged the past and the present, a reminder that the city's mysteries were deep and intertwined with their destinies.

Standing watch over Luminara, Rory knew his journey as the Spectrum Guardian was an ongoing saga that would unfold with each new dawn. He was ready for whatever lay ahead, a guardian of light in a city of endless shadows and boundless mysteries.

Chapter 18

The Veiled Shadows

The encounter with the ancient Guardian profoundly impacted Rory and the city of Luminara. It was a stark reminder of the city's deep-rooted connections to the mystical realm and the responsibilities that came with such powers. For Rory, it was also a personal journey into the legacy of the Guardians, a lineage he was now a part of.

In the wake of the convergence, the city experienced a surge in mystical activity. The awakening of the ancient Guardian had stirred something within Luminara, awakening dormant energies and attracting benign and malevolent entities.

As the Spectrum Guardian, Rory was at the forefront of managing these new challenges. His ability to sense and manipulate the emotional spectrum became crucial in identifying and neutralizing emerging threats.

The team encountered various mystical entities, each presenting unique challenges. Lucas's technical expertise was tested as they dealt with phenomena that blurred the lines between magic and science. Mia's tactical acumen and leadership skills were vital in coordinating their responses to these threats, ensuring the safety of the city's inhabitants.

Aria's knowledge of mystical lore became invaluable as they encountered creatures and situations straight out of the pages of ancient texts. Her ability to decipher old spells and rituals provided the team with the necessary tools to combat the rising tide of magic.

The Shade's network of informants proved essential in tracking the movements of the mystical entities and the various factions vying for power within the city. Their information helped the team stay one step ahead of the unfolding events.

As Rory navigated these challenges, he also grappled with the more profound implications of his role. His encounters with the ancient Guardian had opened his eyes to the vast scope of his responsibilities and the impact of his actions on the city's mystical balance.

Once hidden, the city's magical community became more active in Luminara's affairs. Rory found himself as a mediator, a bridge between the mundane and the supernatural. He worked to foster understanding and cooperation, knowing that the city's future depended on the harmony between these two worlds.

Amidst these developments, a new threat emerged. A shadowy faction, remnants of the Eclipsers, sought to exploit the surge in magical energy. They aimed to seize control of the city's mystical nexus points, harnessing the power for their dark purposes.

The faction was led by a figure known only as the "Veiled Shadow," a master of dark magic whose identity was a mystery. Their influence spread through the city like a dark web, their intentions hidden but undoubtedly malevolent.

Rory and his team embarked on a mission to thwart the Veiled Shadow's plans. They engaged in a series of battles across the city, each encounter bringing them closer to uncovering the true identity of their adversary.

These battles were physical confrontations and tests of will and strategy. The Veiled Shadow was a cunning opponent, their tactics unpredictable and their power formidable.

As they delved deeper into the mystery, Rory discovered a connection between the Veiled Shadow and the ancient Guardian. The Veiled Shadow sought to harness the ancient Guardian's power, using it to open a portal to a realm of darkness.

The final confrontation occurred at one of the city's nexus points, a site of immense magical power. The Veiled Shadow was revealed to be a descendant of the Order of the Veil, seeking to undo the balance of light and dark, plunging Luminara into an age of shadows.

Drawing upon the full spectrum of his powers and the legacy of the Guardians, Rory faced the Veiled Shadow in a climactic battle. The clash of light and darkness was a spectacle that resonated throughout the city, a struggle for the soul of Luminara.

In the end, Rory's light prevailed. The Veiled Shadow was defeated, and their plans foiled. The portal was closed, and the balance of magic in the city was restored.

As peace returned to Luminara, Rory stood atop a building overlooking the city he had sworn to protect. He realized his journey as the Spectrum Guardian was an ever-evolving path filled with challenges and discoveries.

The city of Luminara, with its blend of the mundane and the magical, continued to thrive under his watchful eye. Rory, the Spectrum Guardian, remained its steadfast protector, a symbol of hope and a guardian of the light in a world where shadows always lurked just beyond the corner.

Chapter 19

The Whispering Dark

The defeat of the Veiled Shadow and the stabilization of the mystical energies within Luminara did not mark the end of challenges for Rory and his team. Instead, it heralded a new era in the city, where the line between the mundane and the magical was irrevocably blurred.

In the aftermath of the recent events, Rory found that the city's perception of him had shifted. To some, he was a hero, a beacon of hope in a world that had grown increasingly complex and dangerous. To others, he was a reminder of the unknown, symbolizing the mysteries and powers that now stirred within Luminara.

Amidst this reverence and wariness duality, Rory continued navigating his role as the Spectrum Guardian. His connection to the city and its people deepened, and a heightened sense of responsibility came with it. He knew that every action he took, every decision he made, had far-reaching consequences.

The team, too, found their roles evolving. Lucas became pivotal in integrating advanced technology with the city's newfound magical aspects, creating systems that could monitor and regulate the flow of mystical energies. Mia's leadership skills and strategic thinking were more crucial than ever as they dealt with both mystical threats and the complexities of working alongside the city's authorities.

Aria's expertise in ancient lore and magical history became a beacon for those seeking to understand the new world. Her insights helped in their missions and educated the public, bridging the gap between fear and understanding.

The Shade, ever elusive, played a vital role in informing the team of the undercurrents within Luminara's magical and mundane sectors. Their network of informants became an essential asset in predicting and preventing potential threats.

As Luminara adapted to its new reality, a series of unexplained incidents began. Whispering in the dark, shadows moving at the edge of vision and unease permeated the city. These occurrences were subtle and easily dismissed as imagination or trickery. Still, Rory sensed something more profound, a sinister undercurrent beneath the surface.

Investigating these incidents led Rory and his team to a startling discovery. A new form of darkness was spreading through Luminara, elusive and insidious. Unlike previous threats, this darkness didn't manifest through overt displays of power or intent. Instead, it seeped into the city's fabric, whispering doubts and fears, sowing discord and mistrust.

The source of this darkness was a mystery. It left no trace, no tangible evidence that could be analyzed or combated. It was as if the very shadows of the city had come alive, fed by its inhabitants' lingering anxieties and uncertainties.

Rory's abilities were put to the test. His connection to the emotional spectrum meant he was acutely aware of the shift in the city's mood, the growing sense of fear. He knew he had to find the source of this darkness before it overwhelmed the city.

The investigation took Rory and his team through Luminara's hidden layers. They explored ancient ruins, delved into forgotten archives, and sought the counsel of mystical beings that had remained hidden from the world until now.

Their journey led them to an ancient entity, a being of shadow and silence, forgotten by time. This entity, known as the "Whisperer in the Dark," was a remnant of an age when magic and mysticism were rampant before the balance between light and Dark had been established.

The Whisperer in the Dark had been awakened by the recent surge in mystical energies, its essence seeping into the city. It fed on the people's fears and doubts, growing more robust in the shadows.

Confronting the Whisperer required more than strength; it required understanding the nature of fear and darkness. Drawing upon his experiences and the wisdom of his predecessors, Rory engaged with the entity.

In a realm of shadow and thought, Rory confronted the Whisperer. The battle was not of physical might but of wills, a contest of light and darkness within the mindscape. Rory's resolve, connection to the light, and understanding of the balance between emotions were his weapons in this fight.

After a harrowing and introspective battle, Rory emerged victorious. He managed to contain the Whisperer's influence, sealing it away again in the depths of the city's forgotten history.

As peace returned to Luminara, Rory realized that the battle against the darkness was an ongoing struggle that required vigilance and understanding. With its mix of magic and modernity, the city would always be a place of wonders and dangers.

Standing atop a building, looking out over Luminara, Rory felt a renewed sense of purpose. He was the Spectrum Guardian, the protector of a city where light and darkness danced in an eternal embrace. And as long as shadows whispered in the Dark, he would be there, a guardian of light, a beacon for those who sought hope amid fear.

Chapter 20

The Heart of Light

After the Whisperer in the Dark was contained, Rory's reputation as the Spectrum Guardian became a beacon of hope and stability in Luminara. The city had come to accept the mundane and mystical coexistence. Still, this acceptance brought new challenges and responsibilities for Rory and his team.

With the city's magical heritage now more prominent, various mystical factions sought to establish their influence. This led to a delicate balance of power, with Rory often at the center, mediating and ensuring peace.

With his innovative blend of technology and magic, Lucas developed a network that monitored the city's mystical energies. This network allowed them to predict and preempt potential threats, keeping the city safe from physical and magical dangers.

Mia's role as a strategist and coordinator became even more critical. She liaised with the city's authorities, ensuring a seamless collaboration between their operations and the team's activities. Her leadership was instrumental in bridging the gap between the different worlds within Luminara.

Aria's expertise in ancient lore and deep understanding of magical phenomena made her a respected figure in academic and mystical communities. She held lectures and seminars, educating the public and fostering a better understanding of Luminara's rich heritage.

The Shade, ever enigmatic, maintained their watch over the city's darker corners. Their network of informants was crucial in uncovering hidden threats and keeping the team informed of the undercurrents within the city's mystical underworld.

Despite the relative peace, Rory felt a growing sense of unease. He sensed an undercurrent of subtle but persistent darkness threading through the city. This feeling led him to investigate deeper, delving into the heart of Luminara's mysteries.

His search brought him to an ancient part of the city, where the veil between realms was thin. In the forgotten catacombs beneath the streets, Rory discovered the source of his unease – a breach in the fabric of reality. This fissure led to a realm of pure darkness.

Rory realized that this breach was a remnant of the city's turbulent past, a scar left by the numerous battles and magical upheavals Luminara had experienced. If gone unchecked, this fissure could become a conduit for dark forces seeking to enter the city.

Sealing the breach was daunting. It required Rory's powers and the combined efforts of his team and the mystical communities within Luminara. It was a testament to the unity and strength that the city had fostered.

Lucas engineered a device that could stabilize the breach, while Aria provided the necessary incantations to reinforce the seal. Mia coordinated the operation, ensuring every aspect was meticulously planned and executed. The Shade secured the perimeter, watching for any interference from evil entities.

Rory felt a deep connection with the city and its inhabitants as he worked to seal the breach. He realized that his role as the Spectrum Guardian was more than just protecting the town from threats; it was about nurturing its heart, the light that made Luminara unique.

With effort and determination, the breach was sealed. The operation succeeded, but Rory knew it was a temporary solution. The city's magical heritage and position as a nexus of mystical energies meant such challenges would arise again.

However, Rory also knew that Luminara was resilient. It had faced darkness and uncertainty and emerged stronger each time. As long as he was the Spectrum Guardian, he would be there to protect, guide, and shine a light in the darkest of times.

As he watched over the city, the lights of Luminara twinkling below, Rory felt a sense of pride and purpose. He was more than just a guardian of the town; he was a part of its soul, a symbol of the light that endures even in the deepest shadows.

Chapter 21

The Spectrum of Destiny

After sealing the breach, the city of Luminara entered a period of introspection and growth. Now more aware of the mystical elements woven into the city's fabric, the populace sought to understand and engage with this new reality. For Rory, the Spectrum Guardian, this was a time of profound change and reflection.

The city's magical and mundane communities began to integrate more closely, leading to a renaissance in Luminara. This new era brought a fusion of technology, magic, and culture, creating a vibrant tapestry unique to the city.

Lucas's network became an integral part of the city's infrastructure, monitoring mystical activities and ensuring the balance between the magical and mundane. His innovations were celebrated as a testament to the potential of harmonious coexistence.

Mia, recognized for her leadership and tactical skills, became a liaison between the Guardian team and the city's administration. Her role was pivotal in ensuring that the city's policies and strategies included magical and non-magical citizens.

Aria, as a bridge between the academic and mystical realms, established a center for studying magical arts and history. This center became a hub of learning and discovery, attracting scholars and practitioners worldwide.

The Shade continued their work in the shadows, but their role evolved. They became a guardian of the city's hidden truths, ensuring that the balance of power remained fair and that the darker elements of the mystical community were kept in check.

Amidst this blossoming of culture and understanding, Rory was at a crossroads. His journey as the Spectrum Guardian had taught him much about power, responsibility, and the delicate balance of light and dark. He realized that his role was not just to react to threats but to proactively nurture and protect the harmony within the city.

This realization led Rory to explore more profound aspects of his powers and his connection to the emotional spectrum. He discovered that his abilities were tools for protection and fostering understanding and empathy among Luminara's diverse inhabitants.

As he embraced this broader role, Rory became a symbol of unity, a guardian who defended against the darkness and illuminated the best of what Luminara could be.

However, peace is often a precursor to unseen challenges. A new threat emerged one that was unlike any they had faced before. A mysterious force began to weave its way through the city, one that distorted perceptions and sowed discord, threatening the harmony that Luminara had achieved.

This elusive and complex force seemed to feed on the city's newfound balance, twisting it for its own enigmatic purposes. The nature of this threat was unlike anything Rory and his team had encountered, a puzzle that defied conventional understanding.

The team embarked on a quest to uncover the source of this distortion. Their journey took them through the labyrinthine streets of Luminara, into the heart of the city's mysteries. They encountered enigmas and anomalies that challenged their understanding of magic and reality.

As they delved deeper, Rory began to sense a connection between this new threat and the emotional spectrum he wielded. He realized that this force was a manifestation of the city's collective psyche, a reflection of its inhabitants' fears, hopes, and dreams.

Confronting this force required Rory to delve into the depths of his powers and engage the spectrum of emotions within himself. It was a journey that tested the limits of his abilities and his understanding of what it meant to be the Spectrum Guardian.

Rory faced this manifestation in a climactic encounter in a realm where thought and reality merged. It was a battle of wills, a test of his resolve and his ability to understand and empathize with Luminara's collective consciousness.

Through this trial, Rory emerged with a deeper understanding of his powers and role as the Spectrum Guardian. He realized that his journey was about protecting Luminara from external threats and nurturing its inner spirit, the spectrum of emotions and dreams that defined the city.

The victory was bittersweet, as the encounter left Rory with new questions about the nature of his powers and the future of Luminara. However, it also reinforced his commitment to the city and its people.

As Rory stood watching Luminara, the city alive with a blend of light and shadow, he knew that his journey as the Spectrum

Guardian would continue evolving. He was ready to face whatever the future held, armed with the knowledge that the true strength of Luminara lay in its people, in the spectrum of their experiences and emotions.

With its mix of the magical and mundane, the city continued to thrive, a testament to the enduring power of hope and unity. Rory, the Spectrum Guardian, remained its steadfast protector, a guardian of the city's safety, heart, and soul.

Chapter 22

The Symphony of Souls

In the wake of Rory's victory over the manifestation of the city's collective psyche, Luminara entered an era of introspection and unity. The challenge had brought to light the interconnectedness of the city's inhabitants, both mundane and mystical. For Rory, this victory was not just a triumph over an external threat but also an affirmation of his role as the Guardian of Luminara's soul.

Now more attuned to the emotional spectrum Rory represented, the city began to celebrate its diversity and unity more openly. Festivals and gatherings that blended magic and technology, tradition and innovation, became common, symbolizing the harmony Rory had fought to protect.

Lucas's technological marvels, once a means to combat threats, now enhanced the quality of life in Luminara. His inventions facilitated communication and understanding between the city's diverse inhabitants, creating a network that connected not just places but hearts and minds.

Mia's role evolved from tactician to community leader. She organized events and initiatives that united different city sectors, fostering a sense of belonging and cooperation. Her efforts were instrumental in building bridges across Luminara's varied communities.

Aria's center for mystical studies became a place of pilgrimage for those seeking knowledge and wisdom. It was a space where history met the future, ancient lore was preserved, and new discoveries were made. Aria became a revered figure, a custodian of the city's rich heritage.

The Shade, once a watcher in the shadows, now played a more active role in guiding those who sought to understand the deeper, hidden aspects of Luminara. They became a mentor to many, sharing their knowledge of the city's secrets and the balance between light and dark.

As for Rory, his journey as the Spectrum Guardian became more profound. He realized that his powers were not just a means to protect the city but also a way to connect with its inhabitants. He learned to use the emotional spectrum to understand and empathize with the people of Luminara, becoming a faithful guardian of their hopes, fears, and dreams.

However, peace is often a precursor to new challenges. A mysterious phenomenon began to occur throughout Luminara – individuals from different parts of the city started to experience shared dreams. These vivid and enigmatic visions connected them in a web of collective consciousness.

These shared dreams were beautiful and disturbing, creating a tapestry of emotions and experiences that blurred the lines between reality and fantasy. People from all walks of life were drawn into a shared narrative that hinted at a more profound, hidden truth about the city.

Rory and his team delved into this new mystery, exploring the connections between these dreams and the city's mystical energies. They discovered that the shared dreams were centered around an ancient relic, a long-lost artifact of the Order of the Veil that had resurfaced in the city.

This relic, known as the "Orb of Dreams," was a powerful conduit of emotional and psychic energies. It could link people's subconscious minds, creating a shared dreamscape where their thoughts and emotions intermingled.

While not inherently evil, the team realized that the Orb of Dreams could become a threat if misused. In the wrong hands, it could manipulate the city's collective consciousness, bending reality to its will.

The quest to secure the Orb of Dreams led Rory and his team through a journey across both the physical and dream realms of

Luminara. They encountered dream manifestations of their deepest fears and desires, each challenge bringing them closer to understanding the true nature of the Orb.

In a climactic confrontation within the dreamscape, Rory faced the embodiment of the Orb's power – a being of pure emotion and thought. It was a battle that tested the limits of his abilities, requiring him to harness the full spectrum of his powers and his understanding of the human psyche.

With courage and determination, Rory overcame the challenge, securing the Orb of Dreams and ensuring its power was used for the benefit of Luminara. The shared dreams ceased, but the experience left a lasting impact on the city's inhabitants.

The event brought the people of Luminara closer, and their shared experiences forged a deeper sense of community and empathy. It was a reminder of the city's interconnectedness and of the shared destiny that bound its inhabitants together.

As Rory stood watch over Luminara, the city bathed in the soft light of dawn, he reflected on his journey. He had grown from a guardian of the city's safety to a protector of its heart and soul. His connection to the emotional spectrum had become a means to unite the people of Luminara, to guide them through the symphony of their collective experiences.

With its blend of magic and reality, the city continued to thrive under Rory's watchful eye. He was the Spectrum Guardian, a beacon of light in a world of shadows, a guardian not just of Luminara's presence but of its dreams and aspirations.

Chapter 23

The Luminara Chronicles

The resolution of the shared dreams phenomenon marked a new chapter in Luminara's history. Already a mosaic of magic and modernity, the city began to embrace its identity as a place where the extraordinary was part of everyday life. For Rory, the Spectrum Guardian, this era represented a more profound connection with the city he had sworn to protect.

As Luminara moved forward, the bond between its mystical and mundane communities strengthened. This harmony was reflected in the city's architecture, its culture, and the daily lives of its citizens. Buildings infused with enchantments stood alongside modern structures, streets bustled with a diverse mix of people, and the air was filled with a palpable energy.

Lucas's network, now an essential part of the city's infrastructure, continued to evolve. It monitored mystical activities and became a platform for innovation, blending magic and technology to create solutions for the city's unique challenges.

Mia's role as a bridge between different communities became more prominent. She organized forums and councils that allowed for dialogue and collaboration between various groups within Luminara, ensuring that all voices were heard and represented.

Aria's Center for Mystical Studies expanded its reach, becoming a renowned institution for studying magical arts, history, and the interplay between different realms. It attracted scholars, practitioners, and curious minds from around the world.

The Shade, while still a figure of mystery, began to interact more openly with the city's inhabitants. They offered guidance to those seeking to understand the deeper aspects of Luminara's shadows and were instrumental in uncovering hidden threats.

Rory's connection with the city deepened profoundly. He became a guardian not just of its physical safety but also of its spirit and identity. He worked to maintain the balance between light and Dark, understanding that both were essential to the city's essence.

However, peace was not to last. A new challenge emerged from the depths of Luminara's history – an ancient curse that had lain dormant, now reawakened by the city's flourishing energies. This curse began to affect the city's inhabitants, sapping their vitality and casting a pall over Luminara.

The curse was traced back to an old legend that spoke of a vengeful spirit wronged in the city's early days. This spirit had cursed Luminara, and now, with the city's magical energies at a peak, the curse had reactivated.

The team embarked on a quest to break the curse, which took them through the annals of Luminara's history and into the heart of its oldest myths. They sought the help of ancient beings, delved into forgotten crypts, and unraveled complex magical riddles.

Throughout this quest, Rory's powers were crucial. He used the emotional spectrum to connect with the remnants of the past, to understand the story of the vengeful spirit, and to find a way to appease it. His journey was not only a physical one but also an emotional and spiritual odyssey, testing his understanding of forgiveness, justice, and redemption.

In a climactic ritual held at the site of the spirit's wronging, Rory and his team worked to release the curse. The ritual was a delicate balance of magic, emotion, and historical restitution. It required the collective will of the city's inhabitants, a unified effort to heal the wounds of the past.

The ritual was successful. The curse was lifted, and the spirit found peace. Its long-held anger and sorrow dissipated. Luminara was freed from the shadow of the ancient curse, its people rejuvenated, and its energies restored.

The resolution of the curse solidified Rory's role as the Spectrum Guardian. He was not just a protector but also a healer, a unifier, and a bearer of the city's collective history.

As Luminara celebrated lifting the curse, Rory looked out over the city, a tapestry of light and shadow, magic and reality. He realized that his journey as the Spectrum Guardian was an ongoing narrative intertwined with the city's evolving story.

Luminara, with its vibrant streets and a blend of the mystical and the mundane, continued to thrive under his watchful eye. Rory, the Spectrum Guardian, remained its Guardian, a symbol of the city's resilience and capacity for growth and transformation.

Chapter 24

The Fabric of Time

The lifting of the ancient curse marked a turning point for Luminara. Having faced its past and emerged more robust, the city entered an era of unprecedented growth and harmony. The balance between the mystical and the mundane, which Rory and his team had worked so hard to maintain, now flourished, weaving a vibrant tapestry of life in the city.

As Luminara embraced its new era, Rory, the Spectrum Guardian, reflected on the journey that had brought him here. He had grown from a lone guardian of the city's safety to a symbol of its heart and spirit. His connection with the town had deepened, making him not just its protector but also a part of its very essence.

Lucas's network, now a marvel of magical and technological integration, continued to evolve, becoming more than a monitoring system. It connected the city in ways that fostered creativity, innovation, and community, making Luminara a model for cities worldwide.

Mia's role as a mediator and strategist had expanded. She worked to ensure that the city's diverse communities coexisted in harmony, her efforts instrumental in creating a society where differences were celebrated and mutual respect was the norm.

Aria's center for mystical studies became a beacon of knowledge, drawing in those who sought to understand the mysteries of the universe. Her teachings and research contributed to a deeper understanding of the interplay between different realms and the importance of balance.

The Shade maintained their enigmatic presence and safeguarded the city's hidden truths. They reminded us that even in a city of light, shadows play an essential role, providing depth and contrast.

However, the peace was soon challenged by a new threat that transcended physical boundaries and delved into the very fabric of time. Strange anomalies began to occur throughout the city, and temporal distortions disrupted the flow of time, causing chaos and confusion.

These temporal disturbances were traced to an ancient artifact, a relic from when Luminara was a crossroads for temporal travelers. This artifact, known as the Chrono Loom, had the power to weave and unravel the threads of time.

Rory and his team embarked on a mission to secure the Chrono Loom. This quest took them on a journey through Luminara's timeline. They witnessed the city's history firsthand, experiencing its triumphs and tragedies and evolving from a mystical crossroads to a modern metropolis.

Throughout this journey, Rory's connection to the emotional spectrum proved crucial. He navigated the tides of time, his powers allowing him to remain anchored in the present even as they traversed the past.

The quest led them to confront a group of temporal manipulators who sought to alter Luminara's history for their own purposes. These manipulators were powerful, their mastery of time a formidable force that threatened to unravel the very fabric of reality.

Rory and his team fought to protect the city's timeline in a battle that spanned different eras. The confrontation displayed magic, technology, and strategy, a testament to the team's growth and unity.

Rory, tapping into the full spectrum of his powers, faced the leader of the manipulators in a climactic showdown. The battle-tested his understanding of time, space, and his own abilities.

In the end, Rory's determination and connection to the city prevailed. The Chrono Loom was secured, and the temporal disturbances were corrected. The city's timeline was restored, its history intact but now enriched by the knowledge of what could have been.

The resolution of the temporal crisis reaffirmed Rory's role as the Spectrum Guardian. He was a protector not just of the physical and mystical but also of the temporal integrity of Luminara.

As peace returned to the city, Rory stood atop a building, looking out over Luminara. The city, a blend of different times and cultures, thrived under his watchful eye. Rory, the Spectrum Guardian, remained its steadfast protector, a guardian of its history, present, and future.

Chapter 25

The Echoes of Eternity

The resolution of the temporal crisis brought about by the Chrono Loom solidified Rory's standing as the Spectrum Guardian of Luminara and as a protector of its continuum – a guardian across time. The city, now acutely aware of its place in the tapestry of time, moved forward with a renewed sense of purpose and identity.

In the aftermath, the residents of Luminara developed a deeper appreciation for their history and the delicate interplay between past, present, and future. The city became a living museum where historical preservation coexisted with modern innovation, each aspect enriching the other.

Once focused primarily on the present, Lucas's technological network expanded to include historical archives and temporal data. His systems now served as a means of monitoring and protection and as a gateway to understanding the city's evolution.

Mia took on a new role of cultural preservation and community engagement. She organized events and initiatives celebrating Luminara's rich history, bringing together people from all walks of life to share stories, experiences, and traditions.

Aria's Center for Mystical Studies delved into the research of temporal magic and its implications. It became a place where scholars and practitioners could explore the mysteries of time, contributing to a broader understanding of the universe's workings.

The Shade, ever enigmatic, now also guarded the secrets of Luminara's past. They became a link between the ages, providing insight into the city's evolution and the lessons learned from its history.

As Luminara embraced its newfound role as a temporal nexus, Rory faced new challenges. The city's position at the crossroads of time attracted beings and entities from different eras and realities. Not all of these were benign, and Rory's role as the Guardian grew more complex.

An enigmatic entity known as the Time Weaver emerged. This is being sought to manipulate Luminara's timeline for its own cryptic purposes. The Time Weaver was a master of temporal magic, its powers rivaling even those of the Chrono Loom.

Rory and his team embarked on a mission to confront the Time Weaver, a journey that took them through the swirling eddies of time. They navigated alternate histories, parallel realities, and potential futures, each step bringing them closer to understanding the Time Weaver's motives.

The confrontation with the Time Weaver was a battle of wits and wills. Rory had to use his powers and his understanding of Luminara's spirit. The fight transcended physical boundaries, taking place in the realm of possibilities, where every action could have far-reaching consequences across time.

In a pivotal moment, Rory connected with the Time Weaver emotionally, using the spectrum of his powers to reach a mutual understanding. He learned that the Time Weaver was not an enemy but a guardian of sorts that sought to maintain the balance of temporal forces.

With this understanding, Rory and the Time Weaver reached an accord. The entity agreed to cease its manipulations, recognizing that Luminara's destiny was to be shaped by its inhabitants, anchored in the present even as it honored its past and looked to the future.

The resolution of this conflict marked a new era for Luminara. The city, recognized as a temporal nexus, became a meeting point for beings from different times and realities, seeking to learn and experience the unique confluence of energies.

Having faced and understood the complexities of time, Rory emerged as a more profound guardian. His role transcended the physical and the mystical; he was now a guardian of possibilities, a protector of the city's unfolding story.

As Rory looked out over Luminara, the city's vibrant blend of times and cultures, he knew that his journey as the Spectrum Guardian would continue to evolve. Luminara was more than a city; it was a narrative of endless potential, a story he was honored to be a part of.

Chapter 26

The Veil of Realities

The alliance with the Time Weaver opened new avenues for Rory and the city of Luminara. The town had become a confluence point not only of different times but also of multiple realities. This convergence brought a wealth of knowledge, cultural exchange, and new responsibilities and dangers.

Luminara's status as a nexus of realities attracted visitors from parallel worlds, each with unique cultures and technologies. This influx of interdimensional travelers turned the city into a cosmopolitan hub where diverse realities intersected.

Lucas's network was upgraded to accommodate the needs of these new visitors, ensuring their safe integration into the city's fabric. His systems now included dimensional monitoring tools, allowing him to track and manage the intersections of realities within Luminara.

Adapting to her role, Mia became a diplomat of sorts, facilitating interactions between the city's residents and their interdimensional guests. She organized cultural exchanges and forums that promoted understanding and cooperation among the diverse inhabitants of Luminara.

Aria's Center for Mystical Studies expanded its research to include interdimensional magic and phenomena. It became a gathering place for scholars and practitioners from various realities, eager to share their knowledge and learn from the unique magical energies of Luminara.

The Shade's role evolved into a guardian of the city's dimensional gateways. They monitored the traffic between realities, ensuring that the balance of Luminara was maintained and that no evil entities took advantage of the city's unique position.

As Luminara adjusted to its new role, Rory faced the challenge of safeguarding the city and the delicate fabric of realities that converged within it. His powers as the Spectrum Guardian were tested in ways he had never imagined, adapting to the diverse energies and threats that came with the interdimensional interactions.

A new threat emerged from these intersecting realities – a rift in the fabric of the dimensions. This tear threatened to merge and unravel the various worlds converging in Luminara. This rift was caused by an imbalance in the dimensional energies due to the unregulated travel between realities.

Rory and his team embarked on a mission to seal the rift. This task required them to navigate the complex interplay of different dimensional forces. They worked closely with experts from various realities, each bringing their unique perspective and knowledge to the challenge.

The mission led them through a labyrinth of realities, each affected by the rift differently. They encountered worlds of endless night, realms of pure energy, and dimensions where time flowed backward. In each reality, they learned something new about the nature of the rift and how to seal it.

The confrontation with the rift tested Rory's abilities and understanding of the interconnectedness of all things. He had to use the full spectrum of his powers, channeling the emotional and mystical energies of the various realities to stabilize and eventually seal the rift.

In a dramatic climax, Rory, drawing upon the collective will and strength of the diverse beings affected by the rift, managed to mend the tear in the fabric of dimensions. The rift was sealed, restoring balance to the intersecting realities and safeguarding Luminara's place as a nexus.

The resolution of this crisis solidified Luminara's position as a hub of interdimensional harmony. Now a tapestry of multiple realities, the city continued to thrive under Rory's guardianship. He had become more than the Spectrum Guardian of a town;

he was now a protector of the myriad worlds that intersected within Luminara.

As he stood looking out over the city, its skyline blending different architectural styles and energies, Rory understood that his journey as the Spectrum Guardian was an ever-expanding adventure. Luminara was not just a city but a gateway to infinite possibilities, and he was its Guardian, a beacon of light and balance in a multiverse of endless wonders.

Chapter 27

The Spectrum Unfolds

With Luminara now established as a nexus point for multiple realities, Rory, the Spectrum Guardian, found himself in a constantly evolving world. The city had become a melting pot of cultures, ideas, and magical practices. In this place, the impossible seemed to happen every day.

This new Luminara brought with it unprecedented challenges and opportunities. The city's old and new residents adapted to a life where interdimensional beings walked the streets alongside them, where buildings and landscapes changed as influences from other realities merged with their own.

Lucas's network, initially designed to monitor and manage mystical energies, became an essential tool in managing the city's interdimensional aspects. His systems now included algorithms and sensors capable of detecting and harmonizing the various energies from the different realities, preventing potential conflicts or imbalances.

Mia's role expanded beyond that of a strategist and diplomat. She became a key figure in ensuring the smooth integration of interdimensional visitors into Luminara's society. Her community-building and conflict-resolution efforts were crucial in maintaining the city's harmony.

Aria's Center for Mystical Studies became a universal knowledge hub, attracting beings from across the multiverse. It became a place of learning and exchange, where the mysteries of different worlds were unraveled and shared.

The Shade, once a guardian of the city's darker secrets, now played a critical role in monitoring the dimensional gateways. They ensured that these portals remained secure, preventing any entities with evil intentions from entering Luminara.

As the Guardian of this ever-changing city, Rory's powers continued to evolve. His connection to the emotional spectrum deepened, allowing him to understand and empathize with beings from many realities. He symbolized unity and balance, a guiding light in a city confluence of countless worlds.

However, Luminara's harmony was soon threatened by a new crisis. An entity from a fractured reality, the Discordian, sought to destabilize the city's balance. The Discordian could amplify and manipulate the conflicts and disharmony of the various realities, creating rifts and tensions within Luminara.

Rory and his team faced the daunting task of confronting the Discordian. This entity's power challenged the very fabric of Luminara's harmonious existence, turning allies into adversaries and warping the city's reality.

The battle against the Discordian was not just a physical confrontation but a struggle for the soul of Luminara. Rory had to delve into the depths of his abilities, using the spectrum of light to counteract the Discordian's influence of chaos and dissonance.

The team worked together to counter the effects of the Discordian's powers. Lucas's technology played a crucial role in stabilizing the city's realities. At the same time, Mia coordinated efforts to maintain Order and calm among the populace. Aria provided insights into the nature of the Discordian, using her knowledge to devise strategies to counter its influence.

In a climactic encounter, Rory faced the Discordians in a battle that spanned the various layers of reality. He used his understanding of the emotional spectrum to reach out to the Discordian, seeking to find common ground and resolve the conflict without further destabilization.

Through this confrontation, Rory discovered that the Discordian was being torn apart by the conflicting energies of its fractured reality. In a moment of empathy and insight, Rory managed to help the Discordian find a sense of balance, easing its pain and confusion.

The resolution of this conflict brought a new level of understanding and unity to Luminara. The city's residents, from this reality and others, learned the importance of harmony and the strength of embracing their differences.

Rory, having faced and overcome the challenge of the Discordian, grew in his role as the Spectrum Guardian. He had become a protector not just of a city but of a community that spanned the multiverse, a guardian of the delicate balance between myriad worlds.

As he looked out over Luminara, its skyline a collage of realities and possibilities, Rory understood that his journey as the Spectrum Guardian was an endless path of discovery and growth. Luminara, with its infinite possibilities and challenges, was a testament to the strength and resilience of its people and their Guardians.

Chapter 28

The Tapestry of Worlds

The conflict resolution with the Discordian marked a new era of understanding and cooperation in Luminara. The city, a vibrant tapestry woven from countless threads of realities, thrived under the watchful eye of Rory, the Spectrum Guardian. His role had expanded beyond protecting the city to guarding its multiversal harmony.

Integrating beings from various realities brought about a cultural renaissance in Luminara. Art, technology, and magic intermingled, creating a society that was as diverse as it was unified. Festivals showcasing the traditions of different worlds became regular events, celebrated by all inhabitants with enthusiasm and mutual respect.

Lucas's technological contributions became even more vital. He developed systems that monitored the city's safety and facilitated communication and understanding among its diverse residents. His inventions allowed beings from different realities to interact seamlessly, bridging language, culture, and perception gaps.

Mia, now seen as a leader and unifier, continued her work in fostering community bonds. She organized interdimensional councils where representatives from various realities could voice their concerns and work together towards common goals, ensuring that every inhabitant, regardless of their origin, felt at home in Luminara.

Aria's center for mystical studies became a beacon of learning, attracting scholars from across the multiverse. It served as a place where knowledge was freely shared, and the mysteries of different worlds were unraveled and appreciated.

Meanwhile, the Shade continued to safeguard the city's dimensional gateways. Their role was crucial in maintaining the balance of energies and ensuring that the gateways were used responsibly, preventing misuse or exploitation by evil entities.

As Luminara embraced its role as a crossroads of realities, Rory faced new challenges. The city's unique position attracted not only seekers of knowledge and peace but also those who wished to exploit its confluence of energies for their own ends.

A new threat emerged from the depths of the multiverse – an entity known as the Nexus Marauder. This being sought to control Luminara's gateways, aiming to use the city as a stepping stone for conquering other realities. The Nexus Marauder was powerful, wielding strange and volatile energies, even by Luminara's diverse standards.

Rory and his team embarked on a mission to thwart the Nexus Marauder's plans. This mission was a journey through the city's many layers, testing their abilities and understanding of the delicate balance that held the multiverse together.

The battle against the Nexus Marauder was intense and multifaceted. Rory and his team had to contend with the entity's formidable powers and the disruptions it caused in the fabric of the city's realities.

Lucas's expertise was instrumental in tracking the Nexus Marauder's movements and countering its attempts to manipulate the city's gateways. Mia coordinated the city's defenses, rallying the inhabitants and organizing a united front against the threat.

Aria delved into ancient texts and multiversal lore, seeking knowledge to aid them in their battle. Her research uncovered weaknesses in the Nexus Marauder's armor, giving them an edge in the confrontation.

The Shade played a critical role in the shadows, gathering intelligence and sabotaging the Nexus Marauder's plans from within. Their network of informants and spies was invaluable in this covert aspect of the struggle.

In the final confrontation, Rory faced the Nexus Marauder in a battle that spanned the physical and metaphysical realms. He tapped into the full spectrum of his powers, channeling the energies of Luminara's diverse inhabitants. It was a battle that symbolized the city's unity and strength.

With the combined efforts of his team and the support of Luminara's residents, Rory defeated the Nexus Marauder, safeguarding the city and its gateways. The victory was a testament to the power of unity and cooperation across the multiverse.

In the aftermath, as peace returned to Luminara, Rory reflected on the journey that had brought him here. He had become more than a guardian; he symbolized the city's resilience, a beacon of hope in a world of infinite possibilities.

Luminara, with its ever-evolving landscape of realities, continued to thrive. It was a city where magic and technology, tradition and innovation, coexisted in harmony – a place where the tapestry of worlds was not just a concept but a living, breathing reality.

And Rory, the Spectrum Guardian, stood at the heart of it all, a protector of not just a city but a nexus where countless lives and stories converged. His journey continued an endless path of discovery, protection, and growth in the wondrous multiverse of Luminara.

Chapter 29

Reflections on the Spectrum

In the aftermath of the battle with the Nexus Marauder, Luminara entered a period of healing and reflection. Having witnessed the strength of unity against a formidable foe, the city basked in a newfound sense of community and purpose. For Rory, the victory was more than just a triumph over an adversary; it reaffirmed his role as the Spectrum Guardian and reflected the city's resilience.

The streets of Luminara buzzed with energy as inhabitants from various realities came together to rebuild and strengthen their bonds. The cityscape, a blend of architectural styles from different worlds, stood as a testament to the diverse cultures that had found a home in Luminara.

In the wake of the battle, Lucas focused on enhancing the city's defensive systems. He integrated advanced technology with the mystical energies of Luminara, creating a more robust and adaptive network. His work ensured that the city was better prepared for future threats, whether from this world or beyond.

Mia organized community events and celebrations that brought together beings from different realities. These events were social gatherings and platforms for exchange and understanding, fostering a sense of belonging and mutual respect among Luminara's diverse population.

Aria's mystical studies center became a sanctuary of learning and healing. Here, scholars and practitioners worked together to mend the rifts caused by the Nexus Marauder's incursions. The center also hosted discussions and workshops, delving into the lessons learned from the recent events and how they could be applied to ensure a harmonious future for Luminara.

The Shade, once a solitary figure in the shadows, began to engage more with the city's inhabitants. They shared their knowledge of the hidden realms and the delicate balance of powers, helping to guide the city's journey into its new era.

As for Rory, the aftermath of the battle was a time for introspection. He walked the streets of Luminara, connecting with its people and sharing in their joys and sorrows. His role as the Spectrum Guardian had evolved from a protector to a unifier, symbolizing the city's indomitable spirit.

Atop the tallest tower in Luminara, Rory gazed out over the city in a quiet moment. The skyline, a mosaic of light and color, reflected the vast spectrum of realities that had come together here. He realized that his journey was not just about guarding against threats but also about nurturing the dreams and aspirations of Luminara's inhabitants.

Chapter 30

The Guardian's Horizon

Lucas, having fortified the city's defenses, now works on a project to harness the energy of Luminara's diverse realities to provide sustainable power for the city's future. His work symbolizes the fusion of technology and magic, a testament to the possibilities that arise from unity and innovation.

Mia, as a firmly established community leader, oversees planning a city-wide festival. This celebration, dubbed "The Festival of Realms," is a tribute to the spirit of Luminara, a showcase of the city's rich cultural tapestry. It symbolizes the unity and strength the city has gained through its trials and triumphs.

Aria, at her center for mystical studies, prepares to open a new exhibit that chronicles the history of Luminara and the role of the Guardians. The exhibition is a homage to the past while also looking to the future, encouraging the city's inhabitants to continue exploring and learning from the mysteries of the multiverse.

The Shade, now a more prominent figure in the city's narrative, works quietly in the background, ensuring the balance between the realms remains stable. They continue to mentor those who seek to understand the deeper, hidden aspects of Luminara and its connections to other worlds.

As Rory stands atop the city's highest tower during the Festival of Realms, he looks out over the sea of lights and colors. He sees a city that has survived its challenges and thrived, becoming a beacon of hope and unity in the multiverse. In the faces of the people below, he sees reflections of himself – a myriad of emotions, dreams, and aspirations.

At this moment, Rory realizes that his role as the Spectrum Guardian will constantly evolve as Luminara grows. He understands there will be new challenges, adventures, and lessons to learn. But he also knows that he will face them with the strength and support of the city and its people.

As the sun sets and the festival lights illuminate the city, Rory, the Spectrum Guardian, stands ready for whatever the future holds, a symbol of resilience, unity, and hope in a world of endless possibilities.